Growing Painz

Adapted by **Steve Korté**
Based on the episodes
"Let's Get Serious" by **Michael Jelenic**
and **Aaron Horvath**
"Two Parter: Part One" by **Michael Jelenic,**
Aaron Horvath, and **Ben Gruber**
and
"Two Parter: Part Two" by **Michael Jelenic,**
Aaron Horvath, and **Ben Gruber**

LITTLE, BROWN AND COMPANY
New York   Boston

Copyright © 2017 DC Comics.
TEEN TITANS GO! and all related characters and elements © & ™ DC Comics and Warner Bros. Entertainment Inc.
(s17)

Cover design by Carolyn Bull.

Little, Brown and Company
Hachette Book Group
1290 Avenue of the Americas, New York, NY 10104
Visit us at lb-kids.com

First Edition: May 2017

Little, Brown and Company is a division of Hachette Book Group, Inc. The Little, Brown name and logo are trademarks of Hachette Book Group, Inc.

The publisher is not responsible for websites (or their content) that are not owned by the publisher.

Library of Congress Control Number 2016954134

ISBNs: 978-0-316-54843-4 (pbk.), 978-0-316-54841-0 (ebook)

Printed in the United States of America

LSC-C

10 9 8 7 6 5 4 3 2 1

CONTENTS

CONTENTS

CHAPTER 1

It was late at night. Far at the edge of Jump City stood a military storage building with a large barbed-wire fence surrounding it. But tonight there was a gaping hole in the fence. From deep within the building, a soft thump could barely be heard. Then another, but louder. Suddenly, the door to the building was thrown open. The five members of the H.I.V.E.—a notorious team of super-villains—emerged. Gizmo, the pint-size leader of the group, was the first to appear. Close behind him were Mammoth, See-More, Billy Numerous, and Jinx. Each villain was holding a large radioactive tube. The team members chuckled with delight as they carried the dangerous tubes to a nearby van.

Just then, a harsh voice filled the air.

"This ends *today*, H.I.V.E.," called out the mysterious voice.

The five villains gasped and spun around. Their archenemies, the group of super heroes known as the Teen Titans, were standing nearby. Beast Boy, Starfire, Cyborg, and Raven glared at the villains. The leader of the Titans, Robin the Teen Wonder, took two steps forward. He pounded his fists together as he continued to yell at the H.I.V.E. team.

"*Today*, justice will reign," Robin said triumphantly. "*Today*, evil will…"

BLURRRRRRRRRPH!

Robin was interrupted by the sound of a loud fart. It came from one of the Teen Titans standing behind him.

Robin sighed deeply, cleared his throat, and continued to speak.

"*Today*, evil will fall to its knees. *Today*…"

BLURRRRRRRRPH!

Robin turned around to glare at his teammates. He was annoyed to see that all four of them were giggling.

"*Shh, shh,*" whispered Starfire. "Robin is looking."

Robin turned back to the villains and resumed his speech.

"*Today*, hope for the city is renewed…"

BLURRRRRRRRPH!

Robin spun around again, just in time to catch Beast Boy with his tongue extended far beyond his mouth, creating the loud fart noises. The other Titans were doubled over with laughter.

"Excuse me for just one moment, please," Robin said politely to the five villains, as he slowly backed away to approach his teammates.

"Titans, a word..." Robin said through clenched teeth.

When he was just inches away from the other Titans, Robin started yelling, "How many times do I have to tell you to *not* make fart noises when I am striking fear into the hearts of the enemy and..."

BLURRRRRRRRPHHHHHHHHH!

Beast Boy fell to the ground with laughter. He had just created his best fart sound ever!

Robin shouted, "This is supposed to be the final showdown, and you're *ruining* it!"

Cyborg sighed and said, "Dude, why do you always take yourself so seriously?"

"Yeah, have a laugh once in a while," suggested Raven.

"We are the last line of defense for this city," Robin argued passionately. "And if *we* can't be serious about being super heroes, then who can? It's up to us to…"

WHOOOOOOSH!

Robin was interrupted by the sound of three super heroes zooming above his head. As the Teen Titans stared in astonishment, the grim-faced teenagers flew past them and landed next to the H.I.V.E. villains.

"Wow, it's some of the heroes from Young Justice," said Cyborg. "There's Aqualad, Miss Martian, and Superboy!"

"What are *they* doing here?" asked Robin.

CHAPTER 2

WHAAAAAM!

With one mighty swing of his water dagger, Aqualad laid into Mammoth. The giant villain toppled to the ground.

OOOOOF!

Miss Martian stretched out both her arms and slammed her two giant fists against the heads of Gizmo and Jinx, knocking both of them out of the action.

"Whoa, look how *serious* they are," said Robin with admiration.

TWINKLE!

In the middle of his fight, Superboy glanced over at Starfire and gave her a quick wink.

Starfire blushed and whispered with delight, "*Oooo*...Superboy has the sparkling eye of righteousness!"

Superboy spun around and grabbed See-More and Billy Numerous. With ease, the hero slammed the two evildoers together. He then quickly snapped handcuffs over the wrists of all five villains.

"Wow, none of those Young Justice heroes are even smiling," observed Beast Boy.

"I feel so intimidated," admitted Cyborg. "And I *like* it!"

"Now *those* are real heroes," said Raven admiringly.

Aqualad crossed his arms and glared at the five groaning villains.

"Send these five cretins to our base in the Kratoa Nebula for further investigation," he said to Superboy.

Aqualad paused dramatically, and then he mused, "Something tells me this is only the beginning of our problems with…"

"Hey there, Aqualad!" Robin called out, interrupting Aqualad's grim musing.

Aqualad looked down with annoyance to see that Robin was standing in front of him. Robin's head barely reached Aqualad's mighty pectoral muscles.

"Oh hello, Robin," Aqualad said with an impatient sigh.

"Those were some pretty sweet fighting moves back there," Robin said.

Aqualad ignored the compliment and instead stared off into the distance. A noble expression of self-importance filled his face as he said, "I do what must be done."

"That reminds me of the time I–" Robin began.

"Now, uh, you'll have to excuse me," Aqualad said grimly as he backed away from Robin and glanced at the beeping telecommunications device strapped to his wrist. "It appears that there is an emergency in the Gamma Delta Quadrant that needs my attention."

Robin quickly reached for his Teen Titans cell phone and punched a few buttons. "Cool, cool," Robin said as he peered at his phone's obviously empty screen. "I'll probably head out there, too."

Aqualad snickered in response, muttering under his breath, "Why? Is it on your way to a pie-eating competition?"

Robin frowned and said, "What is *that* supposed to mean?

Before Aqualad could answer, Cyborg and

Beast Boy suddenly appeared on either side of him.

"Did someone say *pie*?!" Cyborg shouted.

"I *love* pie!" Beast Boy howled.

Robin lifted both hands in the air and screamed at his teammates, "Not *now*!"

Beast Boy and Cyborg slowly walked away, glaring at Robin.

"So just *what* did you mean?" Robin demanded.

Aqualad sighed, and then he replied, "I did not wish to say anything, but you and your team have brought nothing but shame to all the *real* super heroes. The Teen Titans are a disgrace."

Robin's mouth fell open in disbelief.

"Hey, you are *way* off base, buddy!" Robin argued. "There's no difference between our teams. We may do things a little differently, but we're both just trying to take down bad guys however we can."

"Is that right?" Aqualad asked skeptically as he extended his hand and pointed. "Take a look over there."

Robin glanced over to the area where the handcuffed H.I.V.E. villains were gathered. Raven and Starfire were quickly undoing the handcuffs that held Jinx.

"*Hurry*, before they see us," Raven whispered.

With Jinx's hands now free, Starfire smiled broadly and asked, "Who is ready for another of the Girls' Night Out celebrations?!"

"Yay!" hollered Raven and Jinx as all three girls jumped into a nearby police car and drove off.

Aqualad frowned and turned to Robin. "Super heroes are supposed to inspire hearts and teach valuable lessons about friendship and life," he lectured.

"We do that...sometimes..." Robin said grudgingly.

Aqualad sneered and said, "You mean lessons like 'Books Can Be Dangerous' or 'What Is Better: Burgers or Burritos?'"

"C'mon," Robin said a bit defensively.

"What's so bad about being a little silly from time to time?"

"I'm all for a good laugh," Aqualad said with a frown on his face. "But the Teen Titans cannot be serious for one single moment. Good day!"

Robin opened his mouth to argue, but Aqualad was already walking away. "Um, okay," Robin said with embarrassment. "Good talk, Aqualad. We'll catch up later. Maybe I'll see you in that…uh…Gamma… Quadrant…um…Delta…place…"

Robin looked around. His Teen Titan teammates and the Young Justice heroes had all departed.

Robin's shoulders slumped, and he let out a very serious sigh.

CHAPTER 3

The next morning was sunny and bright outside Titans Tower, the team's HQ. In the living room, four of the Teen Titans were hanging out on the couch. Beast Boy and Cyborg were locked in a fierce video-game battle. Raven was reading. And Starfire was cuddling with her tiny pet, a mutant moth larva named Silkie.

At the other end of the living room, looking

forlornly out a window, Robin stood alone. He let out a deep sigh and then glanced behind him. No one was paying attention to him. He sighed even more dramatically.

Cyborg looked up from his game controller and asked, "What's up with you, dude?"

Robin shook his head sadly and replied in a raspy voice, "Oh, nothing. I was just thinking about my dead parents." He paused. "So tragic."

The other Titans looked at one another in surprise.

"Whoa! What was that?!" Cyborg asked.

"Yeah, try to keep it light, dude," Beast Boy loudly suggested.

"Where did *that* come from?" muttered Raven.

"I have the sadness now," Starfire said as she wiped a tear from one eye.

Robin frowned and said, "Sorry, I'm just brooding."

He then resumed looking out the window.

"Can you brood in the kitchen, dude?" asked Beast Boy. "And maybe bring me back some pickles and peanut butter?"

Robin stomped his foot on the floor and said angrily, *"No!* I want to brood *here*! And it wouldn't be so bad if the four of you could brood, too!"

Starfire put a hand sympathetically on his shoulder and asked, "Robin, are you down in the dumpster because the real heroes made us look completely inadequate?"

"We are real heroes!" shouted Robin. "But we've *forgotten* all that because you've all become real jokesters! Even Raven!"

Raven looked up from her book and said with surprise, "What are you talking about? I'm no jokester."

"Don't play dumb," Robin said. "I saw your act at the comedy club."

"Oh, yeah," Raven said with a smile. "Some

of those routines were great. Remember this one? 'The good thing about having a demon as my father is being immortal. The *bad* thing is having to deal with him for the rest of my life!'"

As Raven chuckled quietly to herself, Robin continued. "Try all you want, Raven. But you're not funny! None of you are!"

BLURRRRRRRRPH!

Beast Boy's tongue waggled in the air as he emitted a super-loud fart sound. Cyborg, Raven, and Starfire all started giggling.

"Admit it, Robin," said Raven. "We're a little bit funny."

Robin shook his head and replied, "Aren't you tired of being two-dimensional? There's so much more to us. I mean, look at Cyborg. He's half-man and half-machine!"

Cyborg smiled happily and pumped his metallic biceps in the air as he boasted, "I know! Pretty cool, right?"

"*No!* It's not cool at all," argued Robin. "In fact, it should be tearing you apart. Are you a man, or are you a machine?!"

Cyborg's smile drooped and turned into a frown.

"Whoa," he said sadly.

"That's heavy stuff, dude," Beast Boy said sympathetically.

Starfire turned to Robin and asked, "Could not being more serious fracture our team?"

Robin nodded his head and said, "Yes, but that's how we become stronger—by being torn apart and then coming back together!" He slammed his fist into his other hand for dramatic emphasis. "Preferably in front of an epic sunset!"

Starfire just looked puzzled. "I do not understand, Robin," she said.

"Of course you don't, Star," said Robin. "Because you're an alien, and that's *your* struggle!" He then turned to his other teammates and shouted, "You should *all* be struggling!"

Cyborg looked thoughtful and said, "Maybe Robin is right. Aqualad and his friends looked really cool."

"They *sure* did!" agreed Robin.

"And I want a tough face and tight muscles," Beast Boy admitted as he pumped his tiny biceps.

"*Of course* you do!" said Robin.

"I have always wanted to visit the Gamma Delta Quadrant," added Starfire.

"We can interrogate some filthy cretins there *right now*!" Robin said eagerly.

Raven said, "I'd like to say to a villain, *'It's just you and me now…'*"

A smile filled Robin's face as he slowly intoned, "Then let's get…"

"…serious?" asked Beast Boy.

"Serious," added Raven.

"Serious!" shouted Cyborg.

"The serious," agreed Starfire.

SERIOUS!!!!!

All five Titans jumped in the air and pumped their fists together!

CHAPTER 4

Seconds later, a strange transformation took place in Titans Tower. All five Teen Titans magically and instantly changed their appearances. They doubled in size, and their muscles began to bulge and ripple. Robin's neck tensed as he lowered his chin dramatically, glowering and stretching his lips into a tight grimace. Starfire's eyes narrowed, and she opened her mouth wide to display her gnashing teeth. Cyborg's sharp, metallic edges clanked dangerously as he pounded his two giant fists into each other. Raven scowled beneath her hood as an aura of darkness surrounded her. Sharp fangs grew within Beast Boy's mouth, and he let out a menacing growl as long, pointy claws shot out from his fingertips.

Even Silkie doubled in size and started snarling seriously.

"To the rooftop, Titans!" Robin bellowed

in a husky voice. "It's time for us to shout out our action-hero one-liners!"

Each Titan marched grimly up the stairs and stepped out onto the roof of Titans Tower.

"If you're not gonna help, then get out of the way!" shouted Cyborg.

"I work alone," said Raven. "You'll only slow me down."

"I'm saying the one-liner, like a *real* hero," added Starfire.

"There is good, and there is evil, and the line between them is clear!" Robin cried out as he perched dramatically on top of a gargoyle that no one had ever noticed on Titans Tower until now.

"I need to use the potty," admitted Beast Boy.

The other four heroes glared at Beast Boy.

CRUNCH! CRUNCH! CRUNCH!

The next morning, the newly enlarged, amply muscled, and now *very* serious members of the Teen Titans gathered around the kitchen table to eat their breakfast. The only sound to be heard was the five Titans chewing their cereal through gritted teeth. Finally, Robin broke the silence.

"Who here would like to make a silly comment about eating pie?" he angrily demanded of his teammates.

"How can I talk about pie?" grumbled Cyborg. "I've been so conflicted and unhappy all this time, and I never even knew it!"

"Yes, Robin," agreed Starfire with a frown. "There is too much suffering in this world for such merriment."

"You were right, Robin," said Beast Boy with a low growl. "I've never felt more emotionally complex, yo."

"Totally," Raven tersely agreed.

Starfire reached out and grasped Robin's shoulder and said, "I am grateful for what you've done for us, Robin."

Suddenly, Cyborg jumped back from the kitchen table. He proudly pumped his metallic biceps and flexed his pecs.

"Look at how defined my muscles are!" he yelled. "Booyah!"

Beast Boy stretched his mouth wide to form a grimace.

"Wow, I can't even smile anymore!" he boasted.

Robin crossed his thickly muscled arms and struck a triumphant pose.

"Finally, we are no longer disgraces," he said. "We are the team I always dreamed we could be. This, my friends…*this* is what SERIOUS looks like."

"Things just got the real…" Starfire began, and then she gasped. "I am now saying the one-liners just like a real hero!" she said with pride.

All five Titans lifted their heads, crossed their arms over their chests, and planted their feet firmly on the floor. For the next ten minutes, they stood in the middle of the kitchen showing off their most heroic poses.

BREEEEP! BREEEEP! BREEEEP!

The piercing wail of the Titan's crime alert system broke the silence. All five Titans ran into the living room. Robin peered at a video screen.

"The president is calling us to say that H.I.V.E.'s about to launch a murder satellite," Robin said. "If we can't stop them, the world will be destroyed...*forever*!"

The serious looks on the faces of all five Titans grew even more serious.

"Titans, GO!" Robin yelled.

CHAPTER 5

Later that evening, over five hundred miles away from Jump City, the skies grew dark over one of the nation's largest army bases. A ring of mountains surrounded the base. Five grim super heroes stood atop one of those mountains. The Teen Titans peered intently at the army base far below them.

"What are we looking at, Robin?" asked Starfire. "It is very dark."

"Of course it's dark," snapped Robin. "Nighttime is the most serious time to fight crime!"

Raven squinted in the darkness, struggling to view the scene below her.

"Yeah, but I can't see anything, either," she said.

"It makes it even more *dangerous*," Robin said with grim satisfaction.

"I could use my cybernetics to see," Cyborg said, but then he paused to reflect. "Or... would that cause me to lose my humanity?" he wondered.

Beast Boy solemnly faced his teammates and said, "In case we don't come back, I want to say that it's been an honor serving with all of you."

The other Titans nodded grimly.

"It's showtime," Robin said with great seriousness.

An immense domed building stood in the middle of the army base. Inside that building, the five members of H.I.V.E. were busy executing their evil plan to destroy the world. Gizmo was motioning to guide a large crane that Billy Numerous was driving. Mammoth and See-More were looping cables around a giant nuclear missile. Jinx was busy pushing buttons on the control panel of a computer. A large *10* appeared on the countdown clock behind her. Within minutes, H.I.V.E. guided the nuclear missile onto its launching pad.

"Everything is ready," Gizmo announced.

"The missile is good to go!"

CLOMP! CLOMP! CLOMP!

The heavy footsteps of the Teen Titans echoed through the building. The members of H.I.V.E. spun around, surprised.

"No missiles are being launched on *our* watch!" Robin yelled gruffly.

"Whoa, Titans," said Gizmo. "You guys look *serious*!"

"We're *done* playing games with you, H.I.V.E.," Robin said as he heroically placed his hands on his hips.

"Really? That's too bad," said Gizmo. With an evil smile, he reached over and hit a button on the control panel. It was the countdown to launch the missile!

CRASH!

Robin swung his bo staff in the air and

knocked Mammoth to the ground.

10...9...

POW!

Starfire threw a devastating punch to See-More's stomach.

8...7...

ZAP!

Raven emitted a mystical aura that froze Jinx in place.

6...5...

OOF!

Beast Boy transformed into a giant green gorilla and smacked Billy Numerous right in the face.

4...3...

WHAM!

Cyborg pointed his sonic cannon wrist weapon at Gizmo and blasted the villain into the air.

2...1...

WHOOOOOOOOOOSH!

The entire building started shaking as the nuclear missile launched into the air. The Titans watched grimly as the missile shot through an opening in the roof and sailed high above the army base.

"How do we stop it?!" Cyborg asked.

"With *serious* firepower!" Robin yelled. "Titans, GO!"

Within seconds, Cyborg had started reassembling his bionic body parts. He converted his metallic arms into two giant laser cannons. His legs were transformed into powerful jet engines, and his back changed into a passenger cockpit large enough for Robin, Starfire, and Raven to jump aboard.

Meanwhile, Beast Boy morphed into a giant green Tyrannosaurus Rex.

Cyborg and the other Titans quickly latched on to the back of the dinosaur.

ZOOOOOM!

Cyborg's jet engines blasted into action, sending the dinosaur and the other Titans soaring into the air, chasing after the nuclear missile.

ZAP! ZAP! ZAP!

Searing hot blasts shot out of Cyborg's laser cannons. The blasts quickly found their target.

KER-BLAM!

The missile exploded harmlessly in the atmosphere far above Earth. The Teen Titans had saved the planet from certain destruction!

CHAPTER 6

The Teen Titans returned to the army base to gather up the members of H.I.V.E. Suddenly, three figures stepped out of the shadows.

"That was some serious hero work, Titans," said one of the figures.

"Aqualad!" said Robin with surprise.

"We came here to clean up your mess, but it looks like you have everything under control," Aqualad said grudgingly.

Superboy and Miss Martian nodded in agreement.

"Perhaps you can admit you misjudged us," Robin said.

"You do look pretty serious now," Aqualad said. "But I just worry…is it *too* serious?"

"*Too* serious?!" screamed Cyborg. "You don't understand what it's like to be half-machine and half-man!"

"Let's get out of here, Titans," Robin said. "There's a life-and-death emergency in the Muka Muka Sector we have to deal with."

Robin paused dramatically and narrowed his eyes to a squint.

"And something tells me this is only the beginning!" he added, before striding off with extra grim purpose.

44

Twelve hours later, the Teen Titans were back in Titans Tower. Robin was standing next to the window again, lost in deep and very serious thoughts. Cyborg and Beast Boy were sitting at opposite ends of the couch, glaring at each other. Raven and Starfire were seated nearby.

"Can you believe that Aqualad thought we were too serious?" Robin grumbled.

"Not now, Robin," said Beast Boy. "I need to have a little talk with my *supposed* friend, Cyborg."

"What do you mean *'supposed'* friend?" Cyborg asked angrily.

"You know what this is about," declared

Beast Boy. "You drank my juice, and I want to know why!"

"I was thirsty," said Cyborg.

"You *knew* that was my juice! My *name* was on the *carton*!" yelled Beast Boy.

"So?" Cyborg said, stifling a yawn.

"If I can't trust you with my juice, then maybe I can't trust you at all," Beast Boy said, turning away from Cyborg.

"Well, that makes two of us," agreed Cyborg. "Trust is a two-way street, friend-o!"

Robin watched his two teammates with concern. Forcing himself to smile, Robin tried to defuse the situation.

"Hey, guys, let's not get too serious," Robin said. "It was just juice."

"That's easy for you to say," Beast Boy said savagely. "It wasn't *your* juice!"

Suddenly, Raven started yelling, "Guys! The monster in me is feeding on your anger. I don't know who I *am* anymore!"

"C'mon now," Robin said. "You're *Raven*!"

"Am I?" Raven asked with a worried look. A dark aura had surrounded her, and she spun around to confront her teammates. Her face was a mask of pain. "Or am I a *monster*?

Or a *freak*?" she wailed. "I don't think I can be a part of this team anymore!"

"Waaaah!" Starfire burst into tears, and between sobs she asked, "What is happening to our team? Since I have come to this planet, you have been like the family to me. Without the Teen Titans, I have no one."

Beast Boy shouted angrily, "It's too late, Star. He knew what he was doing when he drank the juice. *My juice!*"

"And I enjoyed every single sip of it!" taunted Cyborg.

"Arrrrrgggggh!" screamed Beast Boy as he launched himself into the air and started attacking Cyborg.

"Urrrrrrrggh!" grunted Cyborg as he fought off Beast Boy.

"The darkness is everywhere!" Raven wailed

as an inky blackness surrounded her.

"*Waaaaaah!*" Starfire continued to sob.

Robin surveyed his anguished teammates and pondered quietly, "I thought being serious would bring us closer together, but it's only driven us apart. Could this be the *end* of our team? What will the next chapter bring in the saga of the Teen Titans?"

CHAPTER 7

One chapter later, the Teen Titans were back to their normal sizes and lounging in the Titans Tower living room.

Beast Boy waggled his tongue and made fart noises.

Cyborg rotated his head in 360-degree circles to the sounds of circus calliope music.

Raven reread her favorite *Pretty, Pretty Pegasus* book for the fourteenth time.

Starfire tickled Silkie's tiny pink stomach.

And Robin let out a deep sigh of relief. All of that drama and grimacing was exhausting. So what if they weren't super SERIOUS? At least the team was together.

TWO PARTER: PART ONE

CHAPTER 1

It was a pretty typical Thursday for the Teen Titans. Four of them were lounging in their living room at the top of Titans Tower, their team headquarters. Raven was rereading her favorite *Pretty, Pretty Pegasus* storybook for the fifteenth time. Beast Boy was counting his toes. Cyborg was polishing his metallic chest plate to keep it nice and shiny. And Starfire was cuddling with Silkie, her beloved mutant moth larva.

Suddenly, Robin jumped into the room, startling his teammates. He looked around dramatically.

"Titans! Can you feel it?!" he called out.

Cyborg cautiously took two steps away from Robin.

"No," Cyborg said nervously. "And I don't think I *want* to."

Robin ignored that comment and said, "Well, I can. Something in the air is telling me today is SPECIAL!"

Beast Boy looked up from his toe-counting and asked, "Special how, yo?"

"Special as in something is going to happen that will take twice as long and twice as many pages for us to resolve as it usually does!" Robin said.

Starfire looked impressed. "The increased amount of time *and* pages sounds the amazing!" she said.

"That's right, Star," agreed Robin. "Because ever so often an event occurs that's special—

a special event, if you will—that propels us into an epic adventure!"

Raven glanced up from her book and said in a bored voice, "I'm kinda busy. When does this go down?"

"Any second now," Robin promised. "Just wait for it!"

Seconds passed. Then minutes. As Robin patiently waited, the other Titans shrugged and went back to their tasks.

An hour later, the air conditioner in the corner of the living room gave out a sputtering cough and shut down.

"That's it!" Robin cried out. "Did you hear that? The air conditioning broke down! Talk about *special*!"

"But did we not already experience the breaking of the conditioner of the air long ago?" asked Starfire.

"And that was not special at all," said Raven. "In fact, it was a little boring."

"I'm telling you, this…is…*special*!" Robin insisted. "From this broken air conditioner, we will set forth on our most exciting adventure to date! An extra-long story perhaps divided into two distinct parts! We're talking two separate but linked adventures here, Titans. Who knows… perhaps forty pages for each adventure!"

Beast Boy wiped some sweat off his forehead and sank deeper into the couch. "I'm feelin' pretty hot, yo," he complained.

Robin nodded eagerly and said, "Feeling hot, excellent. Okay! Let's see where our journey continues on our *special* two-part adventure!"

The Titans journeyed to the outdoor swimming pool at the base of Titans Tower. Robin, Raven, Starfire, and Beast Boy had all changed into their swimsuits. They were now floating happily in the pool, splashing in the cool water. Cyborg was standing at the edge of the pool, smiling excitedly at his teammates.

"This does not feel like the special event yet," said Starfire.

"Are you sure?" Robin asked. "Pools can be pretty special!"

"You want something special?" called out Cyborg as he jumped through the air, about to execute a perfect cannonball dive into the pool. *"Caaanooonbaaall!!!!"* he cried out.

Unfortunately, Cyborg's heavy metal body sent him plummeting through the water. He crashed into the concrete floor of the pool and knocked a giant hole in the bottom. The Titans watched with dismay as the water instantly drained from the pool.

"Great job," Raven said sarcastically.

"You ruined the pool, Cyborg!" Robin said, before pausing to add, "Wait, this *could* be special...maybe."

Beast Boy climbed out of the pool and started to walk away.

"Bros, I'm still crazy hot," he said. "I've got to cool off, and I know a special place to do it."

"Did he say *special*?" Robin asked with excitement.

CHAPTER 2

A few hours later, the Titans, still clad in their swimwear, were standing in front of one of the most famous buildings in the world. It was the Hall of Justice, the headquarters of the super-hero team known as the Justice League. The building's shining white towers glinted in the sunlight. In front of the Hall of Justice was a giant fountain filled with sparkling blue water.

Robin turned to Beast Boy and said, "The Hall of Justice? I like where things are going! This is *special*!"

Raven sighed and said, "Please stop saying the word 'special'."

"Just trying to get everyone hyped," Robin explained.

Beast Boy started running toward the giant fountain and called out, "All right, I'm swimming! Who's with me?"

"We are!" yelled Robin, Starfire, and Raven as they jumped into the fountain.

Only Cyborg stood at the edge of the pool, looking worried.

"You know, you guys are disrespecting the fountain with all your horseplay!" he said to his teammates.

Beast Boy splashed some water at Cyborg and said, "Lighten up, bro. C'mon in!"

"No way," Cyborg said. "What if the Justice League catches us?"

"Who cares?" asked Raven.

Cyborg frowned and said, "They would *never* let me join if they caught me swimming in their fountain!"

"I did not know you wished to join the League of Justice," said Starfire.

"It's always been a dream of mine to be part of a *first-rate* super-hero team," Cyborg explained. "I'd give *anything* to be a member of the Justice League!"

Robin was floating on his back as he said, "That's very touching, Cyborg. But you *do* know that if they took anyone, it would obviously be *me*, right? So stop worrying and get in here. It feels great! *Ooooh*…I just found a warm spot in the water!"

Beast Boy smiled at Robin and said, "You're welcome, bro."

"Ewwww!" Raven said as she moved away from Robin.

"What?" asked Robin, puzzled.

"Beast Boy made the water warm," Raven

explained to Robin. "Get it?"

"Well, whatever he did, this warm water is really relaxing my muscles," Robin said as he dipped his head deeper into the water.

"That's the warm embrace of justice, bro," Beast Boy said happily.

Starfire started swimming toward Beast Boy and said, "I also want the embracing of the warm justice."

Raven pulled Starfire out of the fountain and said, "You *really* don't. In fact, we should all get out right now."

"Good idea," said Robin as he climbed out of the fountain. "Since today is so *special*, I think Cyborg should live his dream. Come on, buddy. I'm going to introduce you to the Justice League!"

The other Titans followed Robin to the

front of the Hall of Justice.

"I'm nervous," Cyborg said as he peered up at the hall's immense steel door. "Let's just go home."

"Nonsense, you should meet them," Robin said as he reached up to touch the doorbell. With a chuckle, Robin suspiciously added, "They'll *love* you!"

Cyborg smiled and said, "Do you really think they're going to love—"

Before he could finish his sentence, Robin rang the doorbell and called out, "Uh-oh! Ding dong ditch!"

Laughing hysterically, Robin ran back to the fountain. Starfire, Beast Boy, and Raven were right behind him. "Ding dong ditch! Ding dong ditch!" they all called out as they jumped back into the fountain.

"*No!* Don't leave me!" cried out Cyborg.

The other Titans sank deeper into the water. Cyborg paced nervously in front of the door.

"What do I do? What do I do?" he muttered. "Maybe I can practice introducing myself to the Justice League."

Taking a deep breath, Cyborg faced the closed door, cleared his throat, and smiled broadly.

"Hello…um…hello!" he stammered. "You have a lovely home. Is that jasmine I smell? Greetings! What wonderful capes you have there! Is that one red?"

The other Titans peered over the edge of the fountain and watched their teammate.

"Man, this is boring," said Beast Boy. "No one is even home."

"C'mon, Titans," said Robin as he led them back to the front door. "Since the Hall of Justice is empty, how about a little tour?"

"Yes!" yelled Starfire, Beast Boy, and Raven.

"Noooo!" wailed Cyborg. "Dude, we can't just let ourselves in!"

Robin reached under the doormat and pulled out something shiny.

"Oh, no?" he asked dramatically. "Then why did they leave a *key*?"

71

CHAPTER 3

Inside the Hall of Justice, the Teen Titans craned their necks to admire the mammoth reception area. Marble statues of the team appeared throughout the room. Dozens of display cases held trophies from the team's most exciting adventures.

"Now this truly is a special, special, *special* event," Robin declared.

"You say that, but nothing's actually

happened yet," Raven said.

"But we are filling lots of time…and pages…which is *special*!" Robin replied.

Cyborg stood admiring the statues and trophies. "This *is* special!" he said. "We are in the home of the greatest super-hero team of all time. I feel…inspired!"

"I, too, feel the inspiration!" agreed Starfire.

"So what do you want to see first?" asked Robin.

"Oh, I think you *know* what we want to see first, bro," said Beast Boy with a big smile.

Minutes later, the Teen Titans were gathered together in the kitchen. They stared with awe in front of the open doors of a gleaming stainless-steel refrigerator.

"Of *all* the cool things here, you want to see the *fridge*?!" Cyborg asked in disbelief.

"Somehow...I thought the contents would be more heroic," Starfire said, her voice heavy with disappointment.

Beast Boy quickly grabbed a wrapped sandwich from the refrigerator. "Dibs on the sandwich!" he said as he started peeling off its wrapper.

"No!" yelled Robin. "That belongs to Batman! His name is on it!"

"Come on, bro," Beast Boy said with disdain. "You *really* think Batman cares about a sandwich? Besides, I'm hungry!" Beast Boy took a huge bite out of the sandwich, and suddenly...

BREEP! BREEP! BREEP!

…an alarm filled the Hall of Justice.

"Batman put an alarm on his sandwich?!" Beast Boy said in disbelief as he dropped the sandwich to the floor.

"Of course he did!" said Robin. "He's *Batman*!"

CLANK!

Just then, a large panel in the wall sprang open, and a metal security robot came rolling into the kitchen. At the end of the robot's right arm was a wrist-size laser cannon. The robot moved ominously toward the Teen Titans. "Area restricted to members only," the robot warned as it raised its right arm. "Intruders will be detained."

"You're the tour guide here," Raven whispered to Robin. "What do we do now?"

Robin paused for a moment, and then he said, "There's only one thing to do... *run!*"

He and the Titans frantically tumbled out of the kitchen.

CHAPTER 4

ZAP! ZAP! ZAP!

The angry robot relentlessly pursued the Teen Titans, shooting its laser cannon at the heroes as they ran from one room in the Hall of Justice to another. The Titans somersaulted and jumped through the air to avoid being hit by the robot's laser blasts.

"I've got an idea," Cyborg called out as the Titans ran past an open door. "Follow me!"

Quickly slamming the door shut behind them, the Titans paused to rest for a moment. Looking around, they discovered that they were now standing inside a large locker room. Multiple copies of heroic outfits were dangling from hangers inside the lockers.

Cyborg gathered his teammates around him. "Okay, that robot won't stop for anyone but the Justice League," he said. "So we're going to suit up!"

Robin rolled his eyes and said dismissively, "We're not going to fool the robot by putting on these costumes. What a dumb idea…"

As he said that, Raven dove for the locker that contained Batman's uniform. "Dibs on Batman!" she called out.

Robin jumped in front of her and pulled her away from the locker.

"Slow down there, Raven," he said, "*I'm* Batman!"

POP!

Beast Boy transformed himself into a tiny green bat and flew up to the locker. He grabbed Batman's cape with his tiny, green bat-claws.

"Yo, I can be a bat!" he squeaked. "Let *me* be Batman!"

Starfire rushed over to the locker and declared, "I wish to be the Batman!"

BLAM!

Raven emitted a force field that knocked the other Titans out of the way.

"I already called it! *I'm* Batman!" she said as she slipped Batman's cowl over her head.

Within seconds, her eyes widened with

grossed-out discomfort.

"Ugh, so sweaty," she moaned as she removed the cowl and tossed it to Beast Boy, who had transformed back to his regular body.

Beast Boy sniffed the cowl and grimaced.

"Ugh, it smells like vinegar," he said as he handed the cowl to Starfire.

"And the sweaty cheese," Starfire observed.

Robin stepped up and grabbed the cowl.

"Of course he sweats! He's *Batman*!" Robin said as he slipped the cowl over his head.

"Or should I say...*I'm Batman*!" he declared in his deepest voice, only slightly gagging from the rancid smell of the cowl.

Cyborg handed a small packet of clothing to Beast Boy.

"Beastie, you be Martian Manhunter," Cyborg said.

"Who?" asked Beast Boy.

"You know, the cool green dude from Mars who hunts men all the time!" Cyborg said.

"Sweet! I wanna hunt me some men!" Beast Boy said happily as he slipped into the costume.

Cyborg then handed a star-spangled outfit along with a few accessories to Raven. "You can be Wonder Woman!" Cyborg said.

Raven frowned and said, "Great, so all I get is a swimsuit, some bracelets, and a rope?"

"That rope is the Golden Lasso!" Cyborg declared. "Those bound by it are forced to tell the truth!"

A smile spread on Raven's face as she said, "Oh, really?"

ZIIIIIIP!

The Golden Lasso flew through the air as Raven expertly lassoed Robin.

"Hey, Robin," Raven said. "You remember that wet spot on your pants you said was water?"

Robin struggled within the Golden Lasso. Against his will, he was forced to tell the truth.

"Okay, it was pee!" he admitted. "I said it was water, but it was totally pee. *You* try fighting crime after drinking too much cranberry juice!"

"Cool," said Raven with a contented smile as she quickly unfurled the lasso and freed Robin.

"Who shall I be?" Starfire asked with excitement.

"How about the Flash?" Cyborg asked as he handed her a shiny red outfit.

Starfire quickly donned the Flash's suit, and within seconds she was running around the room. She zoomed up one wall, ran across the ceiling, and then sped down the other wall.

"I am the Flash!" she called out. "Flash! Flash! Flashy Flash!"

Cyborg stepped to the middle of the room. He was now wearing the Green Lantern uniform.

Beast Boy stepped up to him to admire the green ring on Cyborg's right hand.

"Sweet ring, bro!" said Beast Boy.

"This ring is the most powerful weapon in the universe," said Cyborg with pride. "It can manifest anything with the willpower of its bearer. Witness its power!"

Cyborg closed his eyes and started to concentrate. The ring gave off a glow. Suddenly, a blinding green ray shot out of the ring. As the green ray faded away, it was replaced by an elderly lady, glowing green. The woman stood next to the astonished Teen Titans.

"Um, is that a grandma?" asked Raven.

"You know it!" said Cyborg. He reached over to high-five the woman. "What's up, Bea?" he said happily as they slapped their palms together.

Robin shook his head with dismay. "That ring can manifest any weapon imaginable, and you choose a *grandma*?" he asked.

Cyborg looked offended as he said, "This sassy old gal is *the* toughest lady around! When the chips are down, you want a grandma in your corner!"

Robin shook his head and sarcastically said, "Wow, you'd make *such* a great member of the Justice League."

Cyborg turned to the glowing green woman and said, "It's okay, Bea. Not even your sardonic one-liners can make *Robin* a pal and confidante!"

BLAM!

Just then, the robot came crashing through the door. It rolled toward the Teen Titans.

"Okay, now, be cool," Cyborg whispered to his teammates. "Play your parts or this won't work."

"Area restricted to Justice League members

only," the robot warned as it waved the laser cannon on its right arm. "Intruders will be detained."

"Intruders? *Whaaaaat?*" Cyborg said with surprise. "We're the Justice League, baby!"

The robot raised its left hand and emitted a scanning ray that covered Raven from head to toe.

"Scan complete," the robot said. "Welcome back, Wonder Woman."

"Uh, yup. That's me," Raven said with a nervous smile.

"Well, then, we are *clearly* the Justice League," Cyborg declared. "So you can stand down."

The robot turned to Cyborg and ran its scanning device over his body.

"Identity unconfirmed," the robot said.

"State your name."

Cyborg frowned and said, "Green Lantern, *obviously*! Check out the ring!"

"Which Green Lantern?" questioned the robot. "There are several."

Cyborg looked worried.

"What? Why would there be more than *one*?!" he said. "I'm...I'm, you know, uh... Steve?"

The robot again raised its laser weapon and said, "There is no Green Lantern Steve. Intruders will be detained."

ZAP! ZAP!

Suddenly, the robot started firing its laser cannon at every Titan except Raven.

"Yikes!" yelled Cyborg as the Titans jumped through the air, trying to avoid the laser blasts. "Raven, help!"

"Raven? Never heard of her," said Raven as she casually walked back toward the kitchen. "*Hmmm*...I think I'll try one of those yogurts in the fridge."

CHAPTER 5

"*Eeeek!*" yelled the remaining four members of the Titans as they ran out of the room. The robot was right behind them. Starfire hurled energy blasts at the robot, but they bounced harmlessly off its shiny metallic body.

"Uh-oh, dead end coming up," said Cyborg as they turned a corner and reached the end of a hallway. As the robot rolled closer and closer to them, the Titans huddled in the corner, perhaps for the last time.

Robin placed his hand on Cyborg's shoulder.

"Well, Cyborg, you did your best trying to lead us, but we're still going to die," Robin said. "And *that* is why the Justice League would choose *me* over *you* to be in their team!"

"That's *cold*, Robin," Beast Boy observed.

Cyborg let out a deep sigh.

Starfire reached out to hug her teammates and said, "Good-bye, dear friends."

Cyborg suddenly smiled.

"*Friends!* That's it!" he said happily. "Thank you, Starfire. *Thank you for being a friend!*"

Cyborg pointed his power ring directly at the robot. A green ray burst from the ring, and the glowing green image of the old grandma flew from the ring.

"In your face!" yelled Cyborg.

BLAM!

The glowing green fist of Bea smashed into the robot's head. Then she kicked the robot's torso and bashed it with rolling pins. The robot shattered into hundreds of tiny metal fragments.

After their victory, the Titans decided to relax in the Justice League control room. Raven soon joined them, still dressed as Wonder Woman and finishing up her last scoops of yogurt.

"Oh, hey, guys," she said. "How did it go?"

"*Awesome*, that's how!" said Cyborg happily.

Robin smiled and said, "I told you that today was a *special* event!"

"Indeed," said Starfire. "But it took the same amount of time...and approximately the same number of pages...as our other adventures."

BREEEEP! BREEEEP! BREEEEP!

The Hall of Justice emergency alert system began to wail. Concerned, Robin ran to the computer console and read a message on the screen.

"The Justice League has been captured by Darkseid!" he called out to the Teen Titans.

Robin turned to face his teammates. A smile filled his face.

"It looks like this little adventure has

another part coming up," he said with delight. "You know what that means?"

"More pages?" asked Raven.

Robin jumped in the air and yelled, "It means this adventure is going to be… *SPECIAAALLLL!*"

TWO PARTER: PART TWO

CHAPTER 1

As a new chapter opened on Part Two of the Teen Titans' extra-special adventure, the group was gathered around Robin in the Hall of Justice. They were still wearing their Justice League outfits.

"Titans!" Robin announced. "It seems that the second part of this special adventure will entail saving the Justice League from Darkseid!"

"Who?" asked Raven.

Robin quickly pulled up an image on the computer. The scowling face of a monstrous villain known as Darkseid filled the screen.

"Darkseid!" Robin declared. "The most dangerous evildoer in the universe! Vile ruler of the planet Apokolips! Powerful enough to defeat any hero he faces!"

"Even Superman?" asked Cyborg.

"Yes," said Robin.

"Even Batman?" asked Raven.

"Yes," said Robin.

"How about Aquaman?" asked Beast Boy.

"Well, Aquaman wouldn't fight Darkseid," admitted Robin.

"Is it because he is too lazy?" asked Starfire.

"What a bum!" declared Cyborg.

"This totally lowers my opinion of

Aquaman," Raven muttered.

Robin sighed and said, "We have to get to planet Apokolips and save the Justice League from Darkseid's deadly grasp!"

Raven glanced down at the Wonder Woman outfit she was wearing and said, "Fine, but let's change back into our own clothes first."

"No way!" said Cyborg, "We have to wear *these* costumes! To honor the heroes that we aspire to be!"

Raven snickered and said, "Sounds like you want to play dress up and wear your underwear outside your pants."

Cyborg indignantly replied, "I do not! I like my underwear just where it is!"

"Oh yeah?" asked Raven with a smile as she quickly spun the Golden Lasso of Truth and ensnared Cyborg.

Cyborg struggled within the confines of the Golden Lasso and finally admitted, "Okay, I want to play dress up and wear underwear outside my pants! But it's more than that! It's about my dream to join the Justice League. The history...the honor...the justice!"

"In that case," Robin said sarcastically, "I say we all play pretend and act like dumb little babies so Cyborg can live out his childish dream."

"Thanks, Robin!" Cyborg said. "But first, there's one thing I've gotta do..."

Cyborg then shifted into his finest super hero pose—chin lifted, hands on his hips, and legs spread far apart—and declared in a booming voice, "Assembled in the Hall of Justice are the world's greatest heroes! Evildoers beware! These heroes are doing things…everywhere! With their underwear on the outside!"

The other Titans followed Cyborg's heroic example. Each one struck a pose.

Minutes passed.

"Now what?" asked Raven.

"Let's get to our Justice League vehicles," Cyborg declared. "We've got super heroes to save!"

CHAPTER 2

An electronic door slid open and the Titans stepped into the immense garage that contained the Justice League vehicles. They looked around in awe.

Green Lantern's jet floated in the air, hovering a few feet above the red-hued Flash rocket. The black Batwing was parked next to the sleek green-and-purple spaceship that belonged to the Martian Manhunter.

Wonder Woman's invisible jet stood within a large, seemingly empty space in the middle of the garage.

"So we all get our own vehicles?" Beast Boy said with delight. *"Cooool!"*

"I can't wait to try out Wonder Woman's invisible jet," Raven said as she ran up the invisible steps and hopped into the invisible cockpit. Soon, she was waving her hands to shift the jet's invisible controls.

"Okay, let me see…" she said as she pulled an invisible lever.

SKRRRREEECH!

With a violent lurch and the sound of grinding gears, the invisible jet moved backward and slammed into the two vehicles parked behind it. Cyborg and Beast Boy watched with dismay as Green Lantern's jet and the Martian Manhunter's spaceship were smashed into tiny pieces.

"Oops, sorry," Raven said as she pushed an invisible button. "Maybe this one…"

BLAM! BLAM! BLAM!

The invisible plane rolled forward and smacked three times against the Flash's red rocket. Soon, the rocket was a pile of red rubble on the floor of the garage.

"*Oooo*, yikes!" Raven said with dismay. "Okay, okay. I've got it now."

POW!

Within seconds, the invisible jet pulverized the Batwing.

Robin sighed.

"I guess we'll ride with you, then," he said. "Everyone squeeze in."

The other Titans grunted and groaned

as they crammed themselves into the tight confines of the invisible jet. Beast Boy's head was pressed up against Cyborg's back. Starfire's legs were jammed against Raven's neck. Robin had to hang upside-down from the jet's ceiling.

"Ouch," Robin said as his face smacked into Cyborg's elbow. "Okay, let's go."

Raven closed her eyes and reached out to push one more invisible button.

WHOOOOSH!

The invisible jet zoomed through the air. Within seconds, it had emerged from the Hall of Justice and was soaring through outer space.

"Does anyone know the way to Apokolips?" asked Robin.

CHAPTER

3

After several hours and a few wrong turns, the Teen Titans finally landed on the glowing red planet of Apokolips. The Titans looked around apprehensively as they stood on the barren red soil and glanced at the deep red sky above them.

"So this is Apokolips," said Cyborg. "It sure is red." He looked behind him and noticed Beast Boy was missing. "Where's the

Martian Manhunter?" Cyborg asked.

Beast Boy's voice called out from the invisible jet. "Still on the invisible toilet, bro!" he yelled.

"Can you at least shut the door?!" Raven asked angrily.

"You're out of invisible toilet paper, Mama," he said.

"Ew…" muttered Raven.

Cyborg gathered the other Titans around him.

"This is the most dangerous planet in the universe," Cyborg said. "To save the Justice League, we'll have to use all our powers together. Robin, you will have to…" Cyborg looked around. There was no sign of his teammate.

Suddenly, Robin appeared from behind a

red rock. "I'm Batman!" he said.

Cyborg turned to look at him and said, "Listen, I need you to…"

But Robin had vanished again.

"Where'd he go?" Cyborg asked.

Robin dangled upside-down from the invisible jet. "I'm Batman!"

"Listen, I just need…" Cyborg began, but Robin was already gone. *"Stop disappearing dramatically!"* Cyborg shouted.

Robin popped up behind Starfire. "What was that you said?" he asked. "I'm Batman!"

"Stay still and listen!" Cyborg shouted angrily.

But Robin had already disappeared. Seconds later, he appeared on top of Cyborg's shoulder.

"I can't stay still," Robin said. "I'm Batman!"

"Say 'I'm Batman' one more time," Cyborg said ominously. "I dare you. I double-dare you!"

Robin paused. Then he whispered, "I'm. Batman."

Cyborg pointed his power ring at Robin. Suddenly, a glowing green grandma emerged from the ring.

BLAM!

The scowling senior citizen drew back her foot and kicked Robin in the stomach, sending him tumbling through the air.

"Oooooooo!" said Beast Boy. "You just got beat down, son!"

"Thanks, Bea," said Cyborg. "Is there nothing your deadpan sass can't fix?"

Moments later, the Titans nervously approached Darkseid's giant palace. The glowing red building was shaped in the form of Darkseid's scowling face, and the Titans climbed through one of the eyes on the face to enter the palace.

THUMP!

Each Titan dropped as quietly as possible onto the rough stone floor of Darkseid's throne room. They followed a jagged path along the rocky floor that eventually led them to the edge of a steep chasm in the middle of the room. The Titans peered cautiously over the edge of the chasm. Below them was a swirling pool of glowing green acid, violently popping and boiling as evil-smelling fumes wafted in the air.

Cyborg suddenly looked up and gasped. "There! It's the Justice League!" he said.

The other Titans looked up and saw five green metallic pods dangling from chains attached to the ceiling. Each pod was about seven feet long with windows on the sides. With horror, the Titans realized that five members of the Justice League were imprisoned within the pods. It appeared that all five of them were sound asleep. The pods swayed dangerously a few feet above the acid.

"Robin, quick!" yelled Cyborg, "Use your Batarangs to free them!"

Robin reached into his Utility Belt and extracted two Batarangs. He launched them through the air toward the pods.

ZZZZZAP!

Both Batarangs were bombarded with fiery red Omega beams and dissolved into pieces.

Suddenly, the ground shook as a deep, booming voice filled the air. "How dare you enter my home and try to take what is mine?" it shouted.

The Titans spun around and gasped as they beheld the imposing figure of Darkseid. He towered over the heroes and started moving toward them. One hand was stretched out, and his eyes glowed, ready to blast the Titans with more deadly Omega beams!

CHAPTER 4

BLAM! BLAM!

The ground continued to shake as Darkseid's deafening voice filled the room.

"Children should not meddle in the affairs of adults!" Darkseid bellowed, his eyes glowing red as he stepped closer to the Titans.

"That voice...so deep...so *scary*," Robin said nervously.

"So gravelly, yo!" agreed Beast Boy.

Darkseid's voice became even deeper and even more ominous as he thundered, "For your insolence, you will be cast into the fires of…"

Before he could finish his sentence, Starfire flew forward with a small throat lozenge in her hand. "Excuse me, Mr. Seid," she said politely, "but would you care for a lozenge for the scratchies of your throat?"

Darkseid peered down at Starfire and boomed, "Uh, yes, actually, I would. I have been fighting this cold for the *longest* time." He reached for the lozenge, popped it into his mouth, and spent a few minutes sucking on it. He then cleared his throat and spoke again.

"*Mmm*, oh wow! My throat feels *so* much better," he said, his voice no longer dark and booming. In fact, his voice was pleasantly sweet and lyrical. "Thank you!" he chirped.

"My pleasure," said Starfire with a smile.

"Now, where was I?" Darkseid said sweetly. "Oh, yes. You will be cast into the fires of Apokolips, where you will *burn* for eternity!"

The Titans smiled back at Darkseid. Beast Boy even started to giggle.

"Um, you're not cowering in fear," Darkseid observed.

"Your voice isn't threatening anymore," Robin said.

"Oh, c'mon! I'm *still* terrifying," Darkseid said in a whiny, high-pitched voice. "You should be all trembling and stuff!"

"Maybe it'll help if you tell us your evil plans?" offered Raven.

With an evil grin, Darkseid pointed to the pods containing the Justice League members. "Can't you see that I have the lives the Justice League literally hanging in the balance?" he said. "I press a button and *boom*! They're gone!"

"You do not sound like the kind of person

who would do such a thing," Starfire said.

"Well, I'm also going to use the Anti-Life Equation to destroy Earth!" Darkseid added.

Beast Boy laughed and said, "Equations? Are you a bad guy or a math nerd, bro?"

"You know, this dude totally sounds like someone else…" Cyborg said. "Oh! I know! He sounds like Odd Bob!"

The other Titans nodded in agreement.

A look of deep respect came into Darkseid's eyes, as he said, "Ah, yes, Odd Bob. He is the great singer of song parodies. If only I was *half* as evil. To earn a living by making songwriters look like fools! *Diabolical!*"

"I don't know," Cyborg said doubtfully. "I think it's all in good fun."

Darkseid turned to glare at him and said, "What's fun about undercutting musicians by subverting their words and compromising their artistic integrity? Odd Bob is a *true monster!*"

"You take that back!" Cyborg said with a growl. "He is a national treasure!"

"A monster, I say!" declared Darkseid.

"That *tears* it!" Cyborg shouted. "You're going *down*, Darkseid! Justice League, GO!"

Cyborg turned around to see his teammates staring at him with blank looks on their faces.

"That's *you*, guys!" Cyborg said with exasperation.

"Oh, right," said Robin.

"Sorry, bro," said Beast Boy.

The Titans quickly scattered to different corners of the room, hoping to divide Darkseid's attention.

With a burst of Flash-like speed, Starfire

charged directly at Darkseid.

BOOM!

Two fiery red Omega beams shot out of Darkseid's eyes, toppling Starfire to the ground.

Robin fired a grapnel launcher and swung through the air on a borrowed Batcable. He quickly reached into his borrowed Utility

Belt to grab three exploding Batarangs and tossed them at Darkseid. The villain merely smiled as each device exploded harmlessly at his feet.

Omega beams quickly shot out of Darkseid's eyes, severing Robin's Batcable and sending the young hero plummeting to the floor.

CLANG! CLANG! CLANG!

Darkseid blasted three Omega shots toward Raven, who bravely held up her Amazon bracelets to deflect the dangerous rays. With a chuckle, Darkseid watched as one ray bounced off a bracelet and crashed into the floor next to Raven, knocking her to the ground.

"I'm gonna hunt me some man!" yelled Beast Boy as he charged toward Darkseid.

Beast Boy leapt and wrapped his arms around Darkseid's leg and started vigorously chewing on his ankle. Beast Boy's razor-sharp teeth seemed to have no effect on the villain.

Darkseid looked down to glance at his opponent, smiled for a second, and then shot an Omega blast that sent Beast Boy flying across the room.

Now only Cyborg was left standing. Holding his power ring aloft, Cyborg once again created the glowing green image of the mighty grandmother. The feisty lady put her arms on her hips and prepared to face Darkseid.

ZZZZZAPPPPPP!

Darkseid obliterated the golden oldie with a set of Omega beams.

Cyborg fell to his knees in anguish.

"*Nooooo!* You destroyed Bea! How will we ever learn to balance cutting humor and loving friendship without her?!"

Darkseid chuckled as he moved closer to Cyborg, towering over the sobbing hero.

"You failed," said Darkseid. "The Justice League will soon be no more. Earth will be destroyed...along with your precious *Odd Bob!*"

Cyborg frowned and said, "I may have failed as Green Lantern...but I won't fail as Cyborg!"

Cyborg jumped to his feet and removed the power ring from his finger. Instantly, his Green Lantern outfit disappeared. He was once again the hero Cyborg, and he stood defiantly in front of Darkseid.

"Do you really think—" Darkseid began.

But before the villain could finish his sentence, a giant cannon, easily twice the size of the villain, emerged from within Cyborg's mechanical body. The cannon was pointed directly at Darkseid.

"Uh-oh," muttered Darkseid.

KA-BOOOOOOM!

The blast from the cannon thoroughly defeated Darkseid, leaving just his purple boots standing on the edge of the chasm.

"Bull's-eye!" Cyborg said triumphantly.

CHAPTER 5

The other Titans slowly approached Cyborg, who was standing at the edge of the chasm, staring at the dangling metal pods that contained the Justice League.

"You were the amazing, Cyborg!" said Starfire.

"We've never been more proud of you!" declared Robin.

Cyborg smiled and said, "Really?"

Robin pointed to the pods and said, "You defeated Darkseid and saved the Justice League from certain…"

SPLASH!

Before Robin could finish his sentence, the pod containing Martian Manhunter came loose from its chain and dropped into the acid.

"Well, *most* of them," muttered Raven.

Robin watched Martian Manhunter's pod sink into the acid.

"Forget what I just said," Robin muttered. "You're a failure."

"On the bright side, there's a spot open on the Justice League now," added Beast Boy. "You just defeated Darkseid, so they're probably going to take you, bro!"

Cyborg shook his head sadly.

"No, not like this," he said. "I failed them. If only I could reverse time and bring Martian Manhunter back." Cyborg pondered for a moment, and then he said, "Reverse time… that's it! I can send us back in time by flying very fast around the planet, causing it to spin in reverse, creating time travel science."

"You mean like they do in the movies?" Robin asked.

"Exactly!" said Cyborg. "Time travel science!"

"But according to the law of physics…" Starfire began.

"No time to chat," Cyborg said as he launched himself into the air. "Time travel science!" he yelled as he accelerated his speed and starting orbiting the planet.

ZIP! ZIP! ZIP!

Cyborg flew faster and faster around the world. Soon, he was traveling so fast that Apokolips began to rotate backward on its axis. As the planet spun in reverse, time also began to travel backward. Suddenly, it was ten minutes earlier and the pod containing Martian Manhunter was once again hanging from the ceiling of Darkseid's throne room.

As Cyborg returned, Starfire called out, "Quick, save the Martian Manhunter!"

Cyborg reached out to grab Martian Manhunter's pod. Just as he did that, the pod containing the Flash slipped into the acid.

SPLASH!

"Oops," said Cyborg.

Robin pointed to the sky and yelled at Cyborg, "Again!"

ZIP! ZIP! ZIP!

Once again, Cyborg flew into orbit and reversed the planet's rotation. Once again, time retreated ten minutes.

As soon as Cyborg returned to the room, he grabbed on to the pods containing Martian Manhunter and the Flash.

SPASH! SPLASH! SPLASH!

The three pods containing Wonder Woman, Superman, and Batman all slipped into the acid.

"Again!" yelled Robin.

ZIP! ZIP! ZIP!

When he returned this time, Cyborg quickly moved all five pods to the edge of the chasm.

CRASH!

The thin crust at the edge of the chasm gave way, and all five pods tumbled into the acid.

"Again!" yelled Robin.

ZIP! ZIP! ZIP!

Upon his return, Cyborg carefully placed the five pods on thicker ground.

"We did it!" Starfire said happily.

"Let's open these things up!" yelled Beast Boy as he reached to push a button on the nearest pod.

KA-BOOOOOOOM!

All five pods exploded into tiny pieces.

"We are *so* bad at this!" wailed Raven.

"Again," said Robin wearily.

ZIP! ZIP! ZIP!

Once again, Cyborg lugged the five pods to a safe location.

"Let's just leave them here this time," suggested Raven.

"But if we do that, they'll never know that I defeated Darkseid and saved the world!" Cyborg protested.

Starfire put her hand on Cyborg's shoulder and said, "Friend Cyborg, one day the League of Justice will surely recognize your strength and bravery. Just be true to yourself, and you will live your dream."

"Thanks, Star," said Cyborg. "It's always been my dream to be a member of the Justice League! But to think that one day I might be able to call the Hall of Justice my home..."

Cyborg paused, and then he shook his head sadly.

"Huh, like *that* will ever happen," he said.

As Cyborg continued to sigh, the next-to-last chapter of this special two-part adventure came to a close.

CHAPTER

6

Twenty years later, it was finally time for the final chapter in the epic saga of the Teen Titans' special two-part adventure. All things considered, the team held up remarkably well. Beast Boy and Starfire were virtually unchanged. Raven now wore reading glasses. Robin's hairline had receded, and in order to draw attention away from that, he had grown a bushy and rather unattractive mustache.

These four elder Titans gathered outside the Hall of Justice, which gleamed even more impressively than it had twenty years ago.

Robin held a finger in front of his bushy mustache to quiet his teammates.

"Okay, *shhh*," he said as the Titans slowly approached the steel door to the Hall of Justice.

Robin reached out to ring the doorbell.

"This never gets old," he said with a laugh

as the Titans ran to hide behind the fountain.

"Ding dong ditch!" they all called out.

Just then, the Hall of Justice door sprang open, and Justice League team member Cyborg stepped into the sunlight.

"Hey! I see you!" Cyborg said with a smile as he playfully shook his fist in the air.

Cyborg ran toward his former teammates and started chasing the Titans around the fountain.

"Get back here, you scamps!" he said with a laugh.

As the Titans giggled and ran around the fountain, Raven turned to Robin and asked with disbelief, "*This* is the ending for our two-part adventure?"

"I know!" Robin yelled happily. "Talk about *SPECIAL*!"

Turn the page for a

SPECIAL ACTIVITY!

Beast Boy and Cyborg accidentally travel ahead in time and bump into their future selves.

What do the Teen Titans of the future look like?

Don't miss these
TEEN TITANS GO! books.